A Note to Parents and Caregivers:

Read-it! Readers are for children who are just starting on the amazing road to reading. These beautiful books support both the acquisition of reading skills and the love of books.

The PURPLE LEVEL presents basic topics and objects using high frequency words and simple language patterns.

The RED LEVEL presents familiar topics using common words and repeating sentence patterns.

The BLUE LEVEL presents new ideas using a larger vocabulary and varied sentence structure.

The YELLOW LEVEL presents more challenging ideas, a broad vocabulary, and wide variety in sentence structure.

The GREEN LEVEL presents more complex ideas, an extended vocabulary range, and expanded language structures.

The ORANGE LEVEL presents a wide range of ideas and concepts using challenging vocabulary and complex language structures.

When sharing a book with your child, read in short stretches, pausing often to talk about the pictures. Have your child turn the pages and point to the pictures and familiar words. And be sure to reread favorite stories or parts of stories.

There is no right or wrong way to share books with children. Find time to read with your child, and pass on the legacy of literacy.

Adria F. Klein, Ph.D.
Professor Emeritus
California State University
San Bernardino, California

Editor: Christianne Jones
Designer: Joe Anderson
Page Production: Brandie Shoemaker
Creative Director: Keith Griffin
Editorial Director: Carol Jones
The illustrations in this book were created with acrylics.

Picture Window Books
5115 Excelsior Boulevard
Suite 232
Minneapolis, MN 55416
877-845-8392
www.picturewindowbooks.com

Printed in the United States of America.

Library of Congress Cataloging-in-Publication Data
Blackaby, Susan.
New to Drew / by Susan Blackaby ; illustrated by Hye Won Yi.
p. cm. — (Read-it! readers)
Summary: When Drew needs some new clothes, his mother fixes some hand-me-downs,
making them special and "new to him" along with a very special addition.
ISBN-13: 978-1-4048-2417-1 (hardcover)
ISBN-10: 1-4048-2417-0 (hardcover)
[1. Clothing and dress—Fiction. 2. Belongings, Personal—Fiction. 3. Mothers and
sons—Fiction.] I. Yi, Hye Won, 1979- , ill. II. Title. III. Series.

PZ7.B5318Dr 2006
[E]—dc22   2006003580

New to Drew

by Susan Blackaby
illustrated by Hye Won Yi

Special thanks to our advisers for their expertise:

Adria F. Klein, Ph.D.
Professor Emeritus, California State University
San Bernardino, California

Susan Kesselring, M.A.
Literacy Educator
Rosemount–Apple Valley–Eagan (Minnesota) School District

PiCTURE WiNDOW BOOKS
Minneapolis, Minnesota

4

Drew's old clothes did not fit. He needed new clothes.

Mom looked in every room. She found lots of old clothes.

"Your brothers have lots of stuff," she said. "It will be new to you."

Mom patched Jack's old blue jeans.

Mom mended Noah's old blue T-shirt.

Mom sewed a button on the sleeve
of Matt's old red shirt.

Mom fixed the zipper on Danny's old green hooded jacket.

"You are all set," said Mom.

"Everything is new to you."

There was still one problem.

Drew's old shoes did not fit.

Mom looked in every room. She found
lots and lots of old shoes.

But not one of them fit Drew.

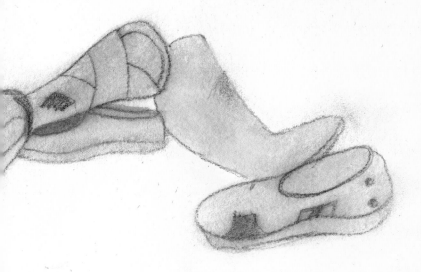

Mom took Drew to the shoe store.

18

19

Drew picked out a pair of red
sneakers. They were the perfect fit.

"Now I am all set," said Drew. "My whole outfit is new to me!"

More *Read-it!* Readers

Bright pictures and fun stories help you practice your reading skills. Look for more books at your level.

Looking for a specific title or level? A complete list of *Read-it!* Readers is available on our Web site:

www.picturewindowbooks.com